Praise for *Past the Glad and Sunlit Season: Poems for Halloween*

"...[K. A. Opperman] is the gifted descendent of poets ranging from Poe to Walter Scott to Robert Burns, all of whom understood that Halloween's deliciously dark mood may be best served by poetry."

— From the Preface by **Lisa Morton**, author of
Trick or Treat: A History of Halloween

"K. A. Opperman's poems evoke both the dark chill of late October and the warmth of a cottage fireside. He captures a time outside of time, an otherworld populated by Pumpkin Kings and haunted souls who wander the edges of our consciousness begging to come inside. The book is a heartfelt incantation to mysteries of Halloween."

— **Lesley Pratt Bannatyne**, author of *Halloween:
An American Holiday, an American History*

"Halloweens past have often been preserved through verse and this collection brings that tradition forward, linking the heritage of old customs with the present and beyond. In the tradition of Burns or Poe, K. A. Opperman's *Past the Glad and Sunlit Season: Poems for Halloween* captures the spirit of the shadow and stirs up deep memories and hidden secrets of this time of the year. These visions of All Hallows' Eve are sure to enchant and whisk the reader away to a world of crisp autumn leaves, brimming with magic. The poems within this collection are steeped in folklore and perfectly reflect the ambiance of Halloween. This book will become your treasured new Halloween tradition."

— **Mickie Mueller**, author of *Llewellyn's
Little Book of Halloween*

"K.A. Opperman has gifted us a varied gathering of lovely, intelligent poems that swell from a passion for the magical black and orange season. Beautiful and evocative, the works are rich in imagery and mood, composed of intriguing rhyme schemes and word choices. Reading this collection made me think of the noble poetry of old, and the subject could not appeal to me more. *Past the Glad and Sunlit Season* is a treasure from a superb wordsmith whose love for the great season burns brighter than a thousand jack-o'-lanterns. I hereby dub Mr. Opperman the poet laureate of Halloween."

— **Scott Thomas**, author of *The Sea of Ash*

"Follow the flickering orange light into the darkness beyond Summer's End, and pay court to the Pumpkin King. . . . K. A. Opperman's passion for Halloween burns as brightly as Jack's fabled lantern. That, combined with his uncanny metrical precision, is a potent recipe for verse-magick that is as haunting as it is darkly delightful."

— **Adam Bolivar**, author of *The Lay of Old Hex*

"*Past the Glad and Sunlit Season* is a cornucopia of autumnal delights. At turns whimsical and sombre, K. A. Opperman's Halloween poems serve as fine evocations of that season of mist, fire, and scythe."

— **Richard Gavin**, author of *Sylvan Dread: Tales of Pastoral Darkness*

"All hail the Pumpkin King, aka K. A. Opperman! Those of us who love Halloween in all its guises will be delighted by this collection of seasonal poetry."

— **Denise Dumars**, author of *The Dark Archetype: Exploring the Shadow Side of the Divine*

Also by K. A. Opperman

FROM HIPPOCAMPUS PRESS

The Crimson Tome
The Laughter of Ghouls (forthcoming)

———————————

FROM JACKANAPES PRESS

October Ghosts and Autumn Dreams:
More Poems for Halloween
(Coming in 2021)

PAST THE GLAD AND SUNLIT SEASON

POEMS FOR HALLOWEEN

PAST THE GLAD AND SUNLIT SEASON
POEMS FOR HALLOWEEN

K. A. OPPERMAN
WITH A PREFACE BY
LISA MORTON

ILLUSTRATIONS BY
DAN SAUER

JACKANAPES
PRESS

"All Hallows' Eve" first appeared in *The Crimson Tome* (Hippocampus Press, August 2015)

"All Souls' Day" first appeared in *Ravenwood Quarterly* No. 2 (Fall 2016)

"The Ballad of Lantern Jack" first appeared in *Order of the Thinned Veil Membership Package* (October 2017)

"The Circus in the Corn" first appeared in *Midnight Under the Big Top* (Cemetery Dance Publications, June 2020)

"The Clown Witch" first appeared in *Midnight Under the Big Top* (Cemetery Dance Publications, June 2020)

"The Darkest Harvest" first appeared in *Hinnom Magazine* No. 9 (November 1, 2018)

"The Darkly Hallowed Day" first appeared in *Hinnom Magazine* No. 9 (November 1, 2018)

"The Fetch" first appeared in *Spectral Realms* No. 8 (Hippocampus Press, Winter 2018)

"Halloween Awaits" first appeared in *Ravenwood Quarterly* No. 2 (Fall 2016)

"The Halloween Mirror" first appeared in *Hinnom Magazine* No. 9 (November 1, 2018)

"Halloween Reverie" first appeared in *Spectral Realms* No. 9 (Hippocampus Press, Summer 2018)

"Halloween Witch" first appeared in *Weirdbook Annual No. 1: Witches* (October 3, 2017)

"The Headless Horseman" first appeared in *Ravenwood Quarterly* No. 3 (Fall 2017)

"Hymn to the Great Pumpkin" first appeared in *The Audient Void* No. 6 (Fall 2018)

"The Jack-o'-Lantern Hearted" first appeared in *Spectral Realms* No. 11 (Hippocampus Press, Summer 2019)

"The Jack-o'-Lantern Trail" first appeared in *Ravenwood Quarterly* No. 2 (Fall 2016)

"Love Beyond the Grave" first appeared in *The Crimson Tome* (Hippocampus Press, August 2015)

"Masque Macabre" first appeared in *Spectral Realms* No. 3 (Hippocampus Press, Summer 2015)

"October" first appeared in *The Crimson Tome* (Hippocampus Press, August 2015)

"The Pumpkin King" first appeared in *The Crimson Tome* (Hippocampus Press, August 2015)

"Samhain Remembered" first appeared in *Ravenwood Quarterly* No. 3 (Fall 2017)

"The Samhanach is Coming" first appeared in *The Audient Void* No. 2 (Fall 2016)

"Séance" first appeared in *Test Patterns* (Planet X Publications, December 23, 2017)

"Thin Grows the Veil" first appeared in *The Crimson Tome* (Hippocampus Press, August 2015)

"The Two Witches" first appeared in *Eye to the Telescope* No. 31 (January 2019)

"Withering Winds" first appeared in *Weird Fiction Review* No. 9 (Centipede Press, January 2019)

"The Wraith" first appeared in *The Crimson Tome* (Hippocampus Press, August 2015)

Past the Glad and Sunlit Season: Poems for Halloween
Copyright © 2020 by Jackanapes Press. All rights reserved.
www.JackanapesPress.com

Poetry, Introduction and Notes copyright © 2020 by K. A. Opperman
Preface copyright © 2020 by Lisa Morton
Cover art and interior illustrations copyright © 2020 by Daniel V. Sauer

Cover and interior design by Dan Sauer
www.DanSauerDesign.com

First Paperback Edition
1 3 5 7 9 8 6 4 2

ISBN: 978-0-578-77105-2

AUTHOR'S DEDICATION

For my mother
For taking us on those twilight walks to see
the glowing pumpkin on the fence

And for my father
For passing on to me the torch of Halloween

—————————

For their encouragement and support in the
release of this book, the publisher would like to thank
Adam Bolivar and Derrick Hussey

CONTENTS

I. ORANGE GLEAMS

II. BENEATH OCTOBER'S MOON

III. TWILIGHT RITES

ILLUSTRATIONS

PREFACE

The night it is good Hallowe'en,
When fairy folk will ride;
And they that wad their true-love win,
At Miles Cross they maun bide.

The lovely lines above date from 1548, appearing in a Scottish version of the traditional folk ballad "Tamlane." The classic poem, which tells the tale of a brave lass who ventures out on Halloween night to rescue her beloved from the Queen of the Fairies, is the earliest recorded mention of Halloween. Over the next three centuries, most references to the holiday would be found in poetry rather than prose.

Halloween, in other words, has its literary roots in poetry.

That's one of the reasons I love this collection. K. A. Opperman has put together a book that reflects not just the true spirit of this ancient festival, but also its fine heritage as a subject for poets.

Look, for example, at these lines from 1584's "Flyting Against Polwart" (I've taken the liberty of updating the spellings):

In the hinder end of harvest, on Allhallow even,
When our good neighbors do ride . . .
The King of Fairy, and his court, with the Elf Queen,
With many eldritch Incubus, was riding that night.

Although the author of this piece, Alexander Montgomerie, actually intended it as a playful jab at a rival, it nevertheless captures the wild romance of that late October evening.

Now compare Montgomerie's lines to these:

The spirit of All Halloween,
A pumpkin with wings like a bat,
At twilight comes wickedly winging,
At call of a witch's black cat.

Those are from this book, written more than four centuries after Montgomerie set quill pen to parchment to set down his words. Notice a similarity?

Or let's talk about the great grandmaster of macabre verse, Edgar Allan Poe. Although Poe's short story "The Black Cat" has become a Halloween staple, in truth it doesn't mention the holiday once, nor does any other fiction of Poe's. But look at this mention from his poem "Ulalume":

For we knew not the month was October,
And we marked not the night of the year—
(Ah, night of all nights in the year!)
We noted not the dim lake of Auber—
(Though once we had journeyed down here)—
We remembered not the dank tarn of Auber,
Nor the ghoul-haunted woodland of Weir.

It's a fair guess that the October "night of all nights in the year" refers to Halloween, and the mention of the "ghoul-haunted woodland of Weir" certainly fits the year's most frightening celebration.

Now read Mr. Opperman's poem "The Wraith," and again, you'll see that he is the gifted descendent of poets ranging from Poe to Walter Scott to Robert Burns, all of whom understood that Halloween's deliciously dark mood may be best served by poetry.

Personally, I think we're lucky to have K. A. Opperman to continue the tradition, although there's a part of me that wonders if he wasn't meant to be here for exactly that purpose.

—Lisa Morton
North Hills, California
13 December 2018

INTRODUCTION

REKINDLING THE JACK-O'-LANTERN FLAME

As a child, I was blessed to fully experience what it is to celebrate the idyllic American Halloween. Every year on the night of October thirty-first, I would step out into the crisp autumn air, cloaked and masked, clutching the hand-sewn treat-bag my grandmother had made for me, and set out to plunder more than my fair share of candy from darkened porches lit by savory smelling, grinning jack-o'-lanterns. This was the only night whereon I was permitted to wander about the dark neighborhood at length, and therefore it was all the more special. Tramping excitedly over the damp, leaf-strewn grass, hopping up each step of every porch, we knocked, or rang the bell, and spoke those magic words: "trick or treat!" Every door that opened was a glimpse into a strange new world—a house we'd never before seen the inside of, and probably never would again—till next Halloween. These were glimpses beyond the everyday—beyond the Veil. Some houses were inviting; some, intimidating with their dark recesses, fake cobwebs, and sinister, mist-shrouded figures leaning near cauldrons of candy, waiting to come to life. But these were the challenges that had to be faced. These were the trials of initiation, whereby we earned our six months worth of candy, and whereby we began to take our first steps toward adulthood.

Amid all of these fond childhood memories, two things stand out as having had an especial impact on me, all these years later. The first was my father's lavish yard display, set up every October without fail. There were foam tombstones with humorous epitaphs painted on them, plastic skeletons, fog billowing up from hidden buckets of dry ice, plastic spiders lurking in cob-webbed bushes, Beistle black cats and witches taped up in the arched windows, and even an alien and his very convincing crashed spaceship, quarantined with caution tape, right on our front yard. Ours was by far the most decorated house in our nook of the neighborhood, and this always made me proud, not to mention filled with excitement for the most sacred night of the year.

The second memory I recall with especial fondness were the twilight walks my mother would take me, my brother and sister on every year to see the jack-o'-lantern blow-mold glowing atop the same fence, alongside a ghost, and possibly a third character. I believe that, subconsciously, this orange beacon whereto we would make pilgrimage helped to solidify in my young heart the dear love for Halloween that I now have today. It was then, I believe, that humankind's most primal veneration for a light in darkness—the Samhain fire's ancient blaze against the pagan night—was atavistically awoken within me. And it may be that this is the underlying reason for Halloween blow-molds' enduring popularity.

Even very early on, I seemed to have quite the predilection for Halloween. During elementary school—fourth or fifth grade—I won a drawing contest wherein we competed to see who could draw the scariest jack-o'-lantern. Mine had worms burrowing from its triangular eyes, spiderwebs over it, and was in general more macabre in appearance than my other classmates were capable of rendering. My prize was a miniature Jack Be Little pumpkin (a variety I have grown myself for the first time this very year), and I bore it home with the utmost pride, a trophy of my sinister accomplishment.

All too soon, however, to my incredible sadness, I found that these enchanted days of gold, and magic autumn nights, were coming to an end. Suddenly, at age fifteen or sixteen, I was too old to trick-or-treat, yet too young to want to stop. I longed for the olden magic of bygone days. I longed, just one last time, to don my costume, and go far off into the night on a nocturnal adventure, in quest of treats, and maybe a little danger. But already I had been getting stares and remarks from the guardians of strange doors, and I knew that my time had passed. At age seventeen, I wandered the darkened streets for one last time, dejected, like a wraith, unable to give up my most precious tradition, but outcast from the groups of excited children who ran from door to door screaming "trick or treat!"

For me, the glad and sunlit season had passed.

* * *

A few years would pass drearily by before, when all others had let it extinguish, I would take up the hallowed torch of Halloween in my own hand. My father was the most proactive proponent of Halloween in the family, so with my parents' divorce quite a few years earlier, a sort of slow decline in our October celebrations had, I think, subtly set in. Aside from that, our living situation changed that December, to a small yet nice house completely sequestered from the street by an imposing brick wall, and thereafter, we would entertain no more trick-or-treaters.

Then one October, something stirred in me. I longed to reclaim the glorious Halloweens of my youth—longed to recapture that fey, magical flame that flickered in smiling pumpkin mouths already fading with time. I was heartsick for a past that had slipped away, as I believe so many of us are. I was finally an adult, a jaded exile, and I wanted my childhood back.

I was sick with an orange-tinged nostalgia.

One fine and sunny autumn day—I must have been about twenty—I boarded the bus and rode it up the street, to visit the local library's little used bookstore in search of cheap horror paperbacks (If I recall correctly, my acquisitions on that trip were a book on the Salem Witch Trials, and a vintage paperback of *'Salem's Lot*.) Almost as an afterthought—at a vague urging rising from the cobwebbed depths of my soul—I decided to quickly procure a pumpkin from the grocery store across the street before I went home—to become the first one I had carved in many years. I stuffed it into my backpack like a severed head, along with my books, and boarded the bus for the ride home. The spirits of Samhain had summoned me to this sacred task; I would once more ignite the Jack-o'-Lantern Flame, when it had been dormant for so many years.

In seven years, when I had attained the age of twenty-four, my living situation was to change yet again. We were forced to relocate to a smaller, older, decidedly less inviting house in a crime-ridden neighborhood. In this house, too, we would bar all trick-or-treaters—the almost none that there were—for fear of attracting any kind of attention in this unsavory part of town. Our quiet celebrations were kept to the inside of the house—but they were there, most assuredly, and I was single-handedly stoking the Jack-o'-Lantern Flame brighter and brighter every year....

After a few years of renewed celebration, during which my instinct toward autumnal festivity began to boil over like a witch's cauldron, my Halloween mania reached fever pitch. I had been contemplating growing my own pumpkins for some time, and when finally I joined a year-round Halloween society and subscription service—the Order of the Thinned Veil, whose members all received a small packet of pumpkin seeds—I finally found the motivation I needed to start growing those beloved gourds. Prior to this, I had never grown or even tended to a single plant in my life, and the experience was quite life changing. I found myself becoming ever more in tune with the cycle of the seasons, the Wheel of the Year, that primal, pastoral foundation on which all of our seasonal celebrations are but haunted way-posts. On September twelfth of that year, my thirtieth birthday—a day I felt was fitting—I harvested the very first self-grown pumpkin of my life.

That year's celebration was to prove especially grand. I hosted my first Halloween party, an intimate gathering in the old-fashioned style, during which games of skill and chance were played, traditional soul-cakes were eaten, and during which we ritually partook of the Harvest, in the form of pumpkin milkshakes I prepared from puree made with a Cinderella pumpkin from my own garden (which, at its height, had been quite formidable, the vines having sprawled across the entire back yard, to eventually produce nearly twenty pumpkins in four different varieties....) The milkshakes, tasting like pumpkin pie in a glass, were quite the hit, and, watched by the impish grins of no less than seven home-grown jack-o'-lanterns, autumnal merriment was had by all. It seemed that I had finally recaptured some of the olden magic from days gone by, only with new and exciting traditions.

The level of Halloween spirit in me had plateaued. I had begun collecting vintage Halloween antiques—mostly postcards and noise-makers—and for a few years now I had begun keeping a year-round Halloween Shrine, a shelf of pumpkin-headed figurines and other autumnal knick-knacks, which I could stand before, in solemn silence, whenever I needed some October-chilled inspiration during the long, long off-months. My deep reverence for, and attunement to, the Hallowed Season, as well as the long, hot summer days of agricultural toil leading up to it, had for me all the poignancy and spiritual fulfillment almost of a religion.

To me, there was no more sacred act than the growing, harvesting, and eventual carving and lighting of a jack-o'-lantern. This virtually year-long ritual, carried out across all four seasons—from planting in spring, to the hard toiling through summer, to the harvesting and carving in autumn, to the burying of rotting remains on the very verge of winter—represented to me the very cycle of life, death, and rebirth, as well as the annual path of the sun through the shifting heavens. The Jack-o'-Lantern Flame was the Sun itself, dying yet glorious, an unquenchable ember, a very beacon of Hope for the New Year, on the other side of the long, dark months to come. Here were the most ancient of chthonic and solar mysteries, seen through the occulting lens of a modern, heavily Americanized, mere children's holiday of spooks, pumpkins, candy-corn, bats and black cats.

I was celebrating the religion of the ancient Celts, albeit in my own particular way, in a new age. I was celebrating the Religion of Halloween.

* * *

Among my other personal Halloween traditions, over the years, it became my custom to write a new Halloween poem every October. Soon enough, however, I found myself writing more and more of them every year, and in every season, and I began to get the notion that maybe I ought to collect a whole book of them. Eventually, as I focused more and more on this goal, such poems came to comprise virtually my entire literary output, for well over a year-long span. In truth, I think I may have maintained this Octobral focus for nearly two years.

And now you hold the book in hand.

I have divided this collection into three sections. The first section, Orange Gleams, contains poems that foreshadow the haunted season beyond summer; poems of longing for autumn, and of October's chill arrival. The second section, Beneath October's Moon, is comprised of poems about the various ghosts, goblins, and other strange characters that come out when the Hunter's Moon rises orange and bright. The third and final section, Twilight Rites, focuses on the day of Halloween itself, its rituals and traditions, and the sad, gray aftermath of the festival as it dissolves into November mists. This is not simply a book of generic spooky poetry, as collections of 'Halloween poetry' so often are. These are poems with a careful and concentrated focus on Halloween itself, and directly related subjects. Some of them are meant merely as seasonal entertainment, but a great many of them, whether in plain speech or veiled symbolism, record my personal ideas, traditions, and philosophies regarding Halloween.

I am now thirty-one years old. I have lived a year for every day in October, my last birthday having been, as I called it, my 'Halloween Birthday.' So it seems that now is a very fitting time for me to be finishing this book.

Once more, I find myself newly settled into a different house—a nice house, in a nice neighborhood—and for the first time since I was seventeen, this year, I was able to decorate the outside of the house, and welcome trick-or-treaters out of the autumn night, as an adult. In many ways, it feels as if I have completed a cycle, and my own initiation into a higher level of the Mysteries. Perhaps I have at last attained the august role of Hierophant.

Dutifully, even as twilight fell, I set out my dimly flickering jack-o'-lantern—grown at the other house, but brought with me to this new stage of life—to greet trick-or-treaters with its jagged goblin grin; that very grin, once guttered to the dimness of memory, but now blazing anew, which had beguiled me as a child, when I had leapt up shadowed steps in perilous quest of candy. I had become the Guardian at the door to the Haunted House, where young aspirants seek for a prize they cannot yet comprehend or grasp, but which, when or if attained, will prove profound indeed, far beyond the immediate boon of candy. I gave them their brightly wrapped sweets, and I showed them the kindness all children deserve, but most importantly, I gave them—if they would have it—a golden key that, one day—perhaps fifty years from now—would lead back through an enchanted door, to this very moment suspended in the mists of time.

There is much hope for the future of Halloween and its venerated traditions. The holiday is now more popular than ever, but it is the children—the trick-or-treaters undergoing that strange twilight pilgrimage, during which they must face the specters of Fear and the Unknown in order to gain their reward—who will keep its most sacred traditions alive; the traditions of pumpkin carving, and of Trick-or-Treat itself. It is they who will stop to stare in awe and wonder at the pumpkin blow-mold softly glowing up on your fence. It is they who will knock on your decorated door, and peer with fear and wonder across the Threshold as you drop the candy into their bags. And it is they who will carry forth the Jack-o'-Lantern Flame, first kindled from ancient Celtic fires, lit in children's hearts by colored plastic lanterns, and finally brought back to blazing life in the sawtooth mouths of hand-carved pumpkins.

It is they who will preserve our precious holiday's olden glory, in the face of a rapidly changing and modernizing world.

It may be that I did some trick-or-treating of my own this year.... It may be that a generous family urged us to take some candy as we strolled by, in awe of the fantastical decorations everywhere we looked, and the countless jack-o'-lanterns flickering darkly on shadowed porches. It may even be the case that I helped myself to several candy bowls left foolishly unattended amidst the imps and devils that prance through the night of All Hallows' Eve....

But concerning these matters, I am sworn to utmost secrecy.

To my amusement, a few people have begun to call me the Pumpkin King. And while I do think there is an obscure and ancient archetype whence the popular idea of this figure has arisen—a looming shadow adumbrated across the fields of summer corn and swelling gourds—I do not think the title can belong to any one man. But I am glad to bear it for as long as readers care to bestow it upon me.

It may be that the glad and sunlit season is over for me now—but I like to think that I have finally found my way back.

— K. A. Opperman
Corona, California
23 November 2018

I

ORANGE GLEAMS

The Orange Book

Take down the book from off the dusty shelf—
Yes, brush away the cobwebs carefully;
A jack-o'-lantern joined by fay and elf
Adorns its orange cover scarefully.

Take down the book of poems, charms, and spells,
Such as enchant in autumn all the more—
The goblin book that in a whisper tells
Of Halloweens of old that went before.

A witch's cackle echoes as you crack
The cover slowly open, to the page
Whereon is writ, in ink of cauldron-black,
A rhyme recalled from childhood's youngest age....

You read the words and travel through the Veil
Back to a haunted, dim-remembered time,
When with a filled and grinning candy-pail,
By candlelight, you read each treasured rhyme.

Halloween Awaits

Past the glad and sunlit season,
Past the solstice, sunlight's treason,
When the shadows drown all reason
'Mid the autumn's red demesne,

Then the jack-o'-lantern's laughter
Flames at twilight, ever after—
Then, the woodland witch will craft her
Haunting spells of Halloween.

Pumpkin Planting

Sow the seeds in fertile soil,
Where it's sunny, where it's warm.
After threat of frost we toil,
Lest our pumpkins come to harm.

Five or six, the farmer's gamble,
Planted half a finger deep.
Water well, with room to ramble;
Pass three months and pumpkins reap.

Chant to the Pumpkin Patch Spirit

Spirit of the pumpkin patch,
Grant to me come harvest time
Pumpkin fruits enough to match
Nature in her autumn prime.

Waiting for October

I'm waiting for October,
The time of Summer's End,
When shadows grow more sober
As apples ripely pend.

I'm waiting for the season
Whose winds are drear and cold—
When without rhyme or reason
Fall leaves of red and gold.

I'm waiting for those moments
When sunlight softly falls—
When Beauty almost torments
My heart in woodland halls.

I'm waiting for the Crescent
To lift her icy scythe,
As acorns rain, incessant,
And nature pays her tithe.

I'm waiting for the gloaming
When gourds and candles glow
To guide the spirits roaming
From lands we cannot know.

I'm waiting for October,
The time of Summer's End,
When shadows grow more sober,
And sorrow is a friend.

Orange Gleams

Through a shifting mist of dream,
Through the months that are to come,
I have glimpsed an orange gleam
'Mid a copse of red and plum—
Gleam of flame in autumn gloaming
An All Hallows' lantern from.

Grinning through the leagues of time,
Gazing straight into my soul,
Terrible and yet sublime,
Jack-o'-lantern, tend your coal,
For too soon will I be roaming
Through your land of death and dole.

The Jack-o'-Lantern Trail

There is a trail that through the woodland wends
When autumn casts her crimson sorcery,
But none can fathom where that pathway ends
Beyond the mist and twilight tracery.

Grim jack-o'-lanterns light the shadowed way,
Each carven visage different from the last;
They flicker over carpets of decay
Where walk the restless spirits of the past.

Soon I will wander down that haunted trail
In search of fleeting, far October dreams,
Against the chill and leaf-arousing gale,
While yet the crescent moon so thinly gleams.

I only know that I shall not return
From where that pumpkin-lanterned pathway ends,
So very deeply does my spirit yearn
To heed the mournful summons that it sends.

Summer's Last Ember

It was painted the first of September,
The pumpkin that once had been green;
An orange like summer's last ember—
The color of All Halloween.

Harvest Moon

For A. D.

We paid a visit to the pumpkin patch
One autumn afternoon,
To see if we could find a prize to match
That evening's harvest moon.

Amid the husks and hay-bales piled up high,
We found our chosen gourd,
Beneath the brilliant blue September sky,
The best in autumn's hoard.

And then we sat beside the sparkling lake
To nod, and doze, and dream;
Deep silence settled in a raven's wake,
The sun a ghostly gleam.

And then we wandered homeward, two as one,
While leaves, like elves, twirled down;
And when the moon, a yellow skeleton,
Uprose, it did not frown.

Jack-o'-Lantern Moon

The moon rose up a pumpkin orange, and peered
Through spooky clouds that crept across the stars.
Upon its disc, a jagged grin appeared—
A jack-o'-lantern carved of lunar scars.

It was a sign of autumn nights to come,
When shadows gather round the ancient blaze;
Red leaves and evenings dyed a deeper plum,
And labyrinths of lost October days.

It was a summons for the most devout
To carve their pumpkins and to worship them—
To never let the hallowed flame go out,
Unless in death they would their souls condemn.

It was an omen that the time was nigh,
And so I knelt beneath the grinning moon,
And with a ghostly, soul-releasing sigh,
Bathed in its beams, I gained October's boon.

The Jack-o'-Lantern Hearted

The jack-o'-lantern hearted,
Whom autumn calls her own,
The all too soon departed,
The lost and the alone,
We know the way to Faerie,
Beyond October's gate,
And we will not long tarry
While twilight grows so late.

The jack-o'-lantern hearted,
The autumn's cursèd kin,
The paramours long parted,
The wan, the worn, and thin,
We know the way to Faerie,
Just down the country lane—
We'll soon be making merry,
And come here not again.

Path of the Will-o'-th'-Wisp

Mine is the path of the will-o'-th'-wisp,
Roaming October's majestical woods;
Mine is the path where the maples grow crisp,
And mushrooms all huddle their hoods.

Mine is the way that no other has gone,
Pathless my footstep, but pointed my tread;
Mine is the way between twilight and dawn,
Where wander the lost and the dead.

Mine is the lantern that mournfully glows,
Carved of a pumpkin and hearted with flame;
Mine is the lantern a trickster once chose,
To follow a fate without aim.

Mine is the path of the will-o'-th'-wisp,
Lost in the autumn, forever astray;
Mine is the path where the maples grow crisp,
With scarlet to carpet my way.

October

Dark time of death, and dreams, and haunted skies,
When trees contort in twisted agony—
When sereing wind so miserably cries—
When all of joy in scarlet tatters lies—
When far-off mists of sorrow witch my eyes,
And all is strange with autumn gramarye.

October lingers near the year's gray tomb
As jack-o'-lanterns cackle wickedly—
As crucified in cornfields, scarecrows loom—
As crow-caws echo through obscuring brume—
As I embrace the specter-shrouded gloom,
And all my soul knows sad tranquility.

Thin Grows the Veil

Thin grows the Veil.... A hush hangs over all.
No scarlet leaf dares twitch in windless air,
Which glows a gold autumnal, mystical,
Seeming to fade as in an aether rare.
Tonight the final twilight will descend,
Like to a shroud upon the dying Year,
Which lies beneath a catafalque of tall,
Majestic oaks whose branches sadly bend.

But as all dies, the olden dead return
As phantom shapes that through the meadows wend,
All through this Hallows' Even to sojourn
Among the living, freed from grave and urn.
And maybe next year's autumn, when once more
The Portal opens, days beyond death's door
Will come again, in ghostly state of yore.

II

BENEATH
OCTOBER'S MOON

The Crows Alone Have Seen

Go not into the pumpkin patch
Whose vines are thick and green;
The scarecrow knows what they would catch—
The crows alone have seen

A farmer vanish in the vines
And nevermore return,
A giant pumpkin showing signs
It had become his urn.

The Patron Wraith of Halloween

The Patron Wraith of Halloween,
With pumpkin head and purple cloak,
Is ruler of the worlds between,
Where spirits pass through mist and smoke.

He wears the candy-corn for crest,
And becks with long and ghoulish claw
To those whom he has darkly blessed,
A jagged grin upon his maw.

—Inspired by a character created by Sam Heimer

The Carver

He carves his pumpkins night and day,
A different grin for every gourd.
In orange guts his fingers play—
But slowly he is growing bored.

He's carven every single face
That from a pumpkin can be made—
The only one he's yet to trace
Is mirrored in his gleaming blade.

He carves his face clean off the skull,
And stitches skin to pumpkin rind;
A candle lights the hollow hull,
The empty sockets blazing, blind.

It is the head of his display,
Which burns beside the rusty barn;
It flickers over corn and hay,
With crisscross grin of rustic yarn.

And yet the Carver cannot cease
To add new lanterns to his ranks.
He'll have no pleasure, rest, nor peace,
Until he fills his trophy-planks.

He dons a jack-o'-lantern mask,
And sews it to his faceless head,
Then sets about his bloody task
With steady, slow, resistless tread.

With pumpkin-spattered knife in hand,
He heads toward the nearest town,
While autumn's moon, so huge and grand
And orange wears a wicked frown.

He wanders down the darkened streets,
In search of grins he's never seen—
That child alone who trick-or-treats
While masked is safe on Halloween.

Lord of Samhain

Enthroned amid the ripened corn,
The Pumpkin King returns, reborn
As Lord of Samhain, till the morn,
When crimson fire will claim him.

He takes the circling crows for crown,
The while the waning sun goes down,
And all around him, sere and brown,
The hissing harvest names him.

'Mid pumpkins paid in solemn toll,
With autumn's moon as aureole,
He feeds upon an offered soul—
The farmer purest-hearted.

Four torches flare upon the field
Where future visions are revealed—
Until at last the Veil is sealed,
And Samhain's lord has parted.

The Pumpkin King

There is a place the hissing shadows shun—
A lonely hill whereto they will not go,
Whose sloping sides are lurid with the glow
Of jack-o'-lanterns—nigh enough to stun
The eye accustomed to the dark of night.
Above the pumpkin-patch that sprawls below,
Enthroned upon its crest, a giant one
Grins wickedly from off its lofty height.

I make obeisance to the Pumpkin King,
Whose evil visage twists in cruel delight
With every bow I reverently make
Unto the mold, where worshipful I cling.
And when at last I slowly stand and take
The downward trail so darkly flickering,
The jack-o'-lanterns titter in my wake.

I Am The Pumpkin King

I roam wherever pumpkins grow
And brambles bear their sting;
Mine is the far and lonely glow—
I am the Pumpkin King.

The jack-o'-lantern is my crown;
The vines upon me cling,
And trail me like a long, green gown—
I am the Pumpkin King.

My kingdom fades at Summer's End;
When midnight's toll should ring
I vanish like an old, old friend—
I am the Pumpkin King.

But when October comes again,
Its misty dreams to bring,
I'll haunt once more the world of men—
I am the Pumpkin King.

The Spirit of All Halloween

The spirit of All Halloween,
A pumpkin with wings like a bat,
At twilight comes wickedly winging,
At call of a witch's black cat.

It grins o'er the ghost-haunted green,
And scatters a candy-corn trail,
A goblin so soon to be bringing
Lost children beyond the thinned veil.

The Ballad of Lantern Jack

I tell the tale of Lantern Jack,
A legend dark and old,
Whose haunting details hearken back
To tales old wives have told.

I tell of old Jack Halloway,
A soldier far renowned
For keeping British troops at bay
By burning captured ground.

One night he led a daring raid
Against a British camp;
From out the forest's midnight shade,
He hurled his flaming lamp....

But during the ensuing fight
A fellow soldier fell,
And onward from that haunting night
Was laid a fatal spell.

The dead man's mother was a witch
Who mourned her son's demise.
She cast a curse as black as pitch,
That Jack from death would rise.

The grave would give no peace, no rest—
He'd roam forevermore,
A mournful revenant oppressed
By horrors of the war.

At Monmouth Jack was sadly slain,
But though he'd bravely fought,
The church, at word of witch's stain,
Refused his corpse a plot.

So fellow soldiers buried him
Beneath a lonesome tomb,
Beside the battlefield grim
Where he had met his doom.

But legend says he will return
At every harvest moon,
In mortal pastures to sojourn
While autumn leaves lie strewn.

With jack-o'-lantern for his head,
And witch-glow in his grin,
He rises from his bloody bed
The while the Veil is thin.

A mass of evil vines that strain
Beneath a war-torn coat,
He hears forever the refrain
Of screams from times remote.

Condemned forever to relive
The tortures of the past,
He waits, though witches won't forgive,
Not till the very last.

The revenant is often seen
To haunt Old Tennent Church,
Or cornfields close Monmouth green—
You'll find him if you search.

But better to remain inside
When Jack is on the roam,
A pumpkin-headed poppet tied
Outside your lighted home.

For only this will fend him off
If one night you should meet.
And if at witchcraft you should scoff,
A simple task complete:

Go plant three pumpkin seeds upon
The grave long overgrown,
And ere All Hallows' Eve has gone,
Jack's lantern will have shone.

—After Jason McKittrick's account of
a New Jersey legend.

The Samhanach is Coming

O child, beware the chilly air,
October twilights numbing;
When leaves fall red and fields are dead—
The Samhanach is coming.

With pumpkin grin and wrinkled skin,
It wakes on Hallows' Even
To roam the night by lantern-light,
A goblin few believe in.

But well you should, for when the wood
At dusk begins to darken,
It takes a child, down elf-roads wild,
Where none to screams can hearken....

O child, take heed of what you read
In books to mold succumbing;
Though known by few, old tales are true—
The Samhanach is coming.

The Headless Horseman

O who is it rides with such thunderous strides
Through woodland and hollow by night?
What goblin or ghost of old legend can boast
A steed of such stature and might?

A Horseman, it's said, who is missing his head
Goes riding down desolate roads
In search of what's lost, and quite high is the cost
Of crossing him—badly it bodes.

To see him uprear on a night dark and drear
'Gainst autumn's magnificent moon,
With pumpkin held high like a head to the sky,
A grin on it wickedly hewn,

Is bad luck indeed, so embolden your steed
If riding by night you must go!
Lest in a dread race should the Horseman give chase—
Then vanish, your soul in his tow....

So if you believe that on All Hallows' Eve
The Horseman is riding abroad,
O hurry back home through the amethyst gloam,
By fireside safely to nod.

It's best to stay in when the night-winds begin
To blow at October's cold dusk,
Lest in the red storm of dead leaves roam his form—
A devil in headless, cold husk.

The Wraith

Last Halloween at twilight strange and gray,
As haunted winds told tales of yesterday,
And crimson leaves blew on their aimless way,
As from an unseen door,
From out the woods a wraith, grave-visaged, old,
Draped in a hooded robe hard to behold,
Came forth to seek amid the windy cold
Some way it knew of yore.

At night it wandered through the ancient town
All wrapped in fog, a huge and ghostly gown.
It found at last the house nigh crumbling down:
Outside, a lonesome flame
Had drawn it forth from death to seek again,
For just one night, a life 'mid mortal men—
But something seemed to vex the spirit then—
Something was not the same.

Where as of old a candle's guiding light
Would welcome home the wraith from autumn night—
A jack-o'-lantern grinned in cruel delight,
And seared it with despair!
Its woeful features crumbled from its face,
Leaving a screaming skull to take their place.
And of that wraith of eld soon not a trace
Was left on misty air.

Masque Macabre

Though I be dead, a body in the ground,
A putrid corpse imprisoned in this cask,
Yet I will dance at my beloved's masque,
Once more to view her gorgeously engowned.

For on the night of Halloween, the dead
Awake and walk beneath October's moon....
O heart that beats defying death's black swoon,
Soon we will quit this sable satin bed....

A crimson plague-mask and a matching cloak
Will serve to veil the dreadful form of death;
A crown of roses, herbs of healthful breath,
Will mask the stench till midnight's fateful stroke.

Thus I will dance away that dreamful night
With my belovèd, in one timeless waltz,
Recalling romance from evanished vaults
That Time had shut forever in his flight.

The orchestra with rich, nocturnal airs,
Will lavish us with song of violins,
And all the masquers, costumed like strange sins,
Will watch us with grotesque, fantastic stares....

But ere the clock strikes twelve I must depart,
Slipping betwixt the scarlet drapes unseen,
Into the night, unkissed by my one queen—
For at that hour, my corpse must drag my heart

Back to the grave to pass a twelvemonth more
Pining for her, imprisoned in the dark.
—I only hope her mourning heart will mark
A passing shadow from the days of yore.

Love Beyond the Grave

On Halloween, when from the Otherworld
The dead are granted one night to return
To living lands, where guiding candles burn,
I visit my belovèd golden-curled.
I watch her weeping through the windowpane,
Her pallid features all with teardrops pearled;
She lays a crimson rose before my urn,
Dreaming of daggers and an end to pain.

Alas, how soon, my love, I must depart,
Not to return until next year! In vain
I strive against the Veil, although my heart
Loves from beyond the grave with wizard art.
And yet as I am drawn back to the land
Of death and dream, through forests grave and grand—
I feel familiar fingers take my hand.

The Fetch

Halloween is drawing nearer,
Pumpkin lamps at twilight glow,
And the attic's antique mirror,
Dim with dust, begins to show
Her angelic face the clearer
As the autumn nights grow drearer,
And her face to me is dearer,
Dearer than I even know.

Halloween is soon returning,
Witches haunt the air unseen,
And my heart and soul are yearning
For the glamored eyes of green
Of the lass I am discerning
In the mirror clearer turning—
Love, or devil, I'll be learning
On the night of Halloween.

The Halloween Mirror

The mirror must contain the gleam
Of moonlight and a pumpkin's glow,
If in it, like a misty dream,
Your future husband's face will show.

An apple, too, must meet your lips,
For taste its red, prophetic fruit
And future's apparition slips
From elsewhere when the owlets hoot.

A witch's silhouette will pass
Across the weirdly shadowed wall....
A ghostly image in the glass
Will watch your knotless tresses fall....

And then his specter will appear
For one brief moment, then to fade
Into a skull with darkling leer—
For Death would marry him a maid.

Séance

The crystal ball reveals an eerie face,
And all the candles flicker, glowing low.
The scarlet curtains flutter with a trace
Of something more than midnight winds that blow.

The tarot cards are scattered—only Death
Remains upturned amid the stars and moons.
The svelte clairvoyant, chilled by spectral breath
Upon her swan-like nape, so nearly swoons.

The ouija board is brought before the host,
And fingers push the planchette here and there.
A message forms, transmitted by a ghost—
The pretty sibyl blanches in her chair....

The skull upon the parlor bookshelf grins
Amid the grimoires, in the gloom unseen;
It knows its mistress and her secret sins,
Revealing all this night of Halloween....

The Clown Witch

With pointed cap of patterned crepe,
And ruffled collar round her neck,
She twirls her skirts where pumpkins gape,
Through rooms that bats and goblins deck.

I follow her throughout the rooms,
Through smoke and weirdly mirrored halls,
Befuddled by the incense fumes,
And watched by blank white stares of dolls.

I pass through black and orange beads,
And find myself in open space;
A path of lamps and lollies leads
Through autumn woods with winding grace.

A horse from some lost carousel
Regards me with a tarnished gleam;
Just where I wander, who can tell—
Some haunted carnival of dream.

A music box, half-buried, plays
Its melancholy melody;
I meet the tiny dancer's gaze—
But hurry past her desperate plea.

At last I find a circus tent,
And through the flaps, I step inside—
And there, above her crystal bent,
The clown witch winks, with grin so wide.

She bids me gaze into the glass,
And with my image I am faced—
But from the crystal's dim morass,
In fragile china fast encased,

There stares a clown of porcelain,
A pierrot with small cap complete—
I am become a manikin,
And 'mid the dolls I take my seat.

The Circus in the Corn

Amid the corn-maze lies a secret circus,
A scarlet tent where cryptic games are played.
The spectral clowns in ruff and dunce-cap shirk us—
This desolation is a strange charade.

The harlequins at night appear and caper,
Tumbling amid the hay-bales, watched by toads;
Beyond the glow of bamboo witch's taper,
A great gray owl sings nocturnal odes.

Beneath the harvest moon, so near the Veil,
When twilight falls, the ghost-white clowns await;
Beneath the Big-Top, past the haunted trail,
A pretty seeress reads the cards of fate....

But now my fancies fade—the sun is setting.
A faint calliope begins to play.
And so we hasten on our way, forgetting
The grinning Fool card found amid the hay.

My Pumpkin Queen

For A. D.

My pumpkin queen,
My pretty witch
With pointed hat
As black as pitch,
The gourd between
Your magic hands
Commands the cat,
And tames the lands.

My pumpkin queen,
Whose greenish gaze
A tilted brim
But half betrays,
On Halloween
You hold my heart,
And nothing grim
Keeps us apart.

Halloween Witch

Astride a broom of birch,
Her flowing hair aflame
Upon the cold October air,
A most enchanting dame,
She races with the bats
Across the autumn moon,
And soars wherever witches dare,
Her song a haunting tune.

She swoops down low to search
The ancient town below,
To find a jack-o'-lantern bright
To lend its grinning glow;
And of the green-eyed cats,
The blackest one will do.
She takes them soaring through the night,
Returning whence she flew.

The Two Witches

There once were two witches and sisters they were,
The one gowned in Orange, the other in Black.
As fire and nightfall that glisters they were,
Primeval opponents that rose to attack.

The Black with a wave of her wand brought the night—
The Orange lit flames on the hilltop and hearth;
In jack-o'-the-lantern she kindled the light,
And will-o'-wisps haunted the swamps of the earth.

The nightfall had failed to extinguish the flames—
But nor could their flickering fend off the dark.
So soon the two witches grew weary of games,
And met 'neath the crescent, the harvester's mark.

On All Hallows' Eve they arrived at a truce:
The Orange would govern the summer's glad realm;
The Black, when the crops would no longer produce,
Would rule over winter when frosts overwhelm.

But both of their banners would hang on that day,
Each color informing October's décor:
Swirled candies and lanterns of papier-mâché;
Black cats and bright pumpkins to deck every door....

And that is the tale of two witches of old,
Two sisters who fought for the rule of the year,
And how black and orange—the story is told—
Became the two colors of Halloween cheer.

III

TWILIGHT RITES

Withering Winds

The withering winds of All Halloween blow
Through trees that the witch-touch of autumn turns red;
The brittle leaves rattle in death's final throe,
And fall in a forest grown heavy with dread.

The withering winds to the scarecrow give voice;
They hiss through the husks and the stuffing of straw.
Who crosses the cornfield at dusk has no choice
But face this grim specter with sharp orange maw.

The withering winds through the windowsill wail,
And claw at the candle to snuff its dim flame.
They bear from a tree-branch that sways in the gale
A skeleton's creaking, the gallows' grim claim.

The withering winds of All Halloween blow,
So turn to the warmth of the spice-scented hearth;
For out in the twilight where pumpkin-lamps glow,
The dead alone wander through woodland and garth.

The Darkest Harvest

We wend our way across the field
In solemn silence, pagan prayer.
The darkest harvest is revealed
As twilight starts to witch the air.

The orange gourds allure our gaze
With promise of the perfect lamp—
A pumpkin lamp whose goblin blaze
Will guide us on our homeward tramp.

By toad and toadstool, snake and mouse,
We choose the fruit that is our fate.
There looms a farmer's darkened house;
The eve is growing very late.

And so we make our slow return
Across the dim and haunted land,
And bear, as if it were an urn,
Our jack-o'-lantern held in hand.

Samhain Remembered

Of all my family, only I remember
The rustic rites of haunted Samhains past.
With ghostly candle, I ignite the ember
That burns against the pagan darkness vast.

Alone, I carve the jack-o'-lantern yearly,
Out of a pumpkin picked with sacred care,
And as at twilight autumn winds blow drearly,
I watch it glow, and meet its ancient stare.

The Altar of Gourds

Bow low before the altar of the gourds,
For they are emblems of the autumn's rule;
They are the gifts the fertile earth awards
To the devout, who delve with hand and tool.

Bow low before the pumpkin and the squash,
Strange fruits engorged with magic of the land,
For wheresoe'er they're gathered grows awash
With witchery the chosen understand.

Hymn to the Great Pumpkin

O orange gourd, great emblem of our Day,
All-hallowed pumpkin, pride of Halloween,
Your shell alone is fit to house the sheen
Of candlelight that keeps the imps at bay.

We've chosen you to hold the Samhain Flame,
And guard against the ghosts that haunt this night.
Yours is the weirdly dancing, eldritch light
Wherein is mystery without a name.

You smile upon the autumn-littered lawn
When in the evening twilight parts the Veil
With spectral hands; you brave the night's travail
With glowing gladness lasting till the dawn.

The trick-or-treaters seek you one by one
To learn a secret some will take to heart.
You are the Hierophant; you play your part
Throughout our lives—your work is never done.

We worship you on porch, in pumpkin patch,
Showing our dear devotion with our toil.
How solemnly we till the summer soil...
How lovingly we carve, and light the match....

You give yourself unto the carver's knife
Year after year, hanged king of Harvest Home.
But though you rot into the autumn loam—
You rise again in spring with green new life.

But we grow old, and spring returns no more,
And then we place you on an ancient porch.
You are the bearer of Tradition's torch,
And you will teach our children ways of yore.

O orange gourd, great emblem of our Day,
All-hallowed pumpkin, pride of Halloween,
When autumn comes for me, I'll walk between
Dim life and death, with you to show the way.

Hallowed Powers

The hallowed powers whisper through the trees,
Awakening with every gust and sigh.
These are the dark and ancient sorceries
The Celts respected 'neath the purpling sky.

These were the forces feared at Summer's End,
When druids gathered round the Samhain flame,
With only masks and costumes to defend
Against the spirits that no grave can tame.

The jack-o'-lanterns cast their shadow-shapes
Like ghosts and witches over autumn lawns,
While in the windows, glimpsed through rustic drapes,
The rites of harvest last till morning dawns.

October's embers fade through blackened boughs,
An orange glamour strong as any spell,
And as the darkness falls, I make my vows—
To serve the hallowed powers true and well.

Masks

The pumpkins wear a wicked mask
This hallowed night, and so will I.
I must complete a sacred task
As twilight winds begin to sigh.

I must confront the Face of Fear
In all its ghoulish, grinning forms—
The cackling witch's yellow leer,
The ghost that moans in autumn storms.

This devil visage makes me brave,
A mask as red as apple-skin,
And though the dead shrug off the grave,
I wander onward, sweets to win.

I stand, a masked initiate,
Before the haunted house's test,
And with three words propitiate
The grinning gourds that greet each guest.

This very doorway is the Veil—
For none have seen the other side;
I rap the brass, to no avail—
But then the ancient door swings wide....

A man emerges from the gloom,
Who wears the shadowed mask of years.
In robes like Samhain flames abloom,
He welcomes me as midnight nears.

He gives to me my share of treats,
And sternly nods, without a word.
I feel the chill of one who greets
A strange, old friend in dream-lands blurred....

The pumpkins wear a wicked mask
This hallowed night, and once did I.
In jack-o'-lantern light I bask—
Until my younger self comes nigh.

The Darkly Hallowed Day

The darkly hallowed day is here,
When faded sunlight strangely falls—
When pumpkins everywhere appear,
And crows all make their mournful calls.

I wander home, bewitched by dreams,
A scarlet crunch beneath my tread.
The very air an omen seems—
I hear the whispers of the dead.

I hasten, for the shades of dusk
Begin to gather in the sky.
The world has all become a husk
Through which the wind begins to sigh.

I hasten, for I must prepare
For twilight's rite of trick-or-treat,
When jack-o'-lantern fires will flare
Along this autumn-haunted street.

The Four Trick-or-Treaters

A witch, a devil, ghost, and skeleton
Went out one Halloween
In search of mischief, mystery, and fun,
And everything between.

They made a pumpkin-lamp to light their way,
A fifth and grinning friend.
They were the players in an ancient play
This night of Summer's End.

They went from door to door demanding treats,
And sometimes playing tricks.
They filled their bags with apples, nuts, and sweets,
Till low burned candles' wicks.

And at the last they wandered slowly home,
Past pumpkins' darkened gleams,
Lamenting that this night would no more come,
Save in their dearest dreams.

Halloween Greetings

If you should see a pretty witch
Sweep past the crescent moon,
Your orchard's yields will be rich,
And marriage will come soon.

The devils, love, are out in droves
This tricksy, wicked night!
So if you go through haunted groves,
Use jack-o'-lantern's light.

A ghost has risen from the grave,
The lonely ghost of yore,
And if this night you don't behave,
He'll greet you at your door.

It's luck to meet a skeleton,
In spite of what they say;
They'll show you awful lots of fun,
And dance the night away.

May jack-o'-lantern light your way
This haunted Halloween,
And cast a laughing, yellow ray
On secrets yet unseen.

When the Owl Takes Flight

When the owl takes flight on All Halloween night,
The message it brings us is clear—
That the dead are abroad where the willow trees nod,
And specters are everywhere near.

When the owl takes wing and the tambourines ring,
You know that the Veil has grown thin;
Now the witch casts her spell, there are fortunes to tell—
The games are about to begin.

Halloween Party

The pumpkin-patterned tablecloth
With grinning gourds is neatly laid;
In quiet corners, mouse and moth
Awaken in the candle-shade.

A festive banner hangs above,
Proclaiming Happy Halloween.
This is a night for youth and love—
And for the ancient things unseen.

Such tricks and treats are had by all
This night of mask and mystery.
They heed a dim, ancestral call,
Though scarce they know the history.

They heed the day of Summer's End,
As all their folk have done before;
And though the trappings are pretend—
They sense the olden ghost of yore.

Jack-o'-Lantern Chant

Jack-o'-lantern, jack-o'-lantern,
Goblin grin of yellow light,
Jack-o'-lantern, jack-o'-lantern,
Frighten off the ghosts tonight.

Jack-o'-lantern, jack-o'-lantern,
In the darkness burning bright,
Jack-o'-lantern, jack-o'-lantern,
Flicker till the morning light.

Jack-o'-Lantern

Jack-o'-lantern burning bright,
Light my way this Hallows' Eve.
Witches take their moonlit flight,
Devils their deceptions weave.

Jack-o'-lantern burning true,
Guide me through the graveyard gate.
All my heart is filled with rue,
And the year is very late.

Halloween Reverie

With every Halloween
That sadly goes a-passing,
The autumn leaves amassing
On lawns that once were green,
I know I'm growing older—
The poignant purple smolder
Of sunset burns more keen
On Halloween.

With every Halloween
That vanishes in shadows
While glow the twilight meadows
With jack-o'-lantern sheen,
The summer fades behind me—
I hope that you will find me
In some far, dim demesne
On Halloween.

All Hallows' Eve

A wraith of eld goes wandering this night,
From out hesternal autumns, through the mist,
Lonely and lost, its only guiding light
A single coal that hell has hardly missed.

So too the youth I was so long ago
Goes off to wander through a phantom past,
Whose jack-o'-lanterns still yet faintly glow
Amid dim dreams that sadly could not last.

Visions From Beyond the Veil

An owl takes wing above the sleepy town,
And sweeps by windowpanes where pumpkins glow—
Toward the woods where crooked oak trees frown,
And autumn winds through shadowed branches blow.

In orange robes, twelve cultists now convene
Around a single jack-o'-lantern's light.
They are the guardians of Halloween,
And they will keep the ancient faith tonight.

A Dia de los Muertos maiden stands
Draped with a serpent where the owl alit.
Guitars and horns, with blackest sarabands,
Bring her to dance as graveyard-flames are lit.

Soon a black cat past jack-o'-lanterns slinks,
Toward a hollow oak, to disappear,
And as the crescent moon, so scythe-like, sinks,
The Queen of Witches sleeps, until next year.

All Souls' Day

The jack-o'-lanterns rot, and fungus grows
Inside the shriveled caverns of their grins.
The darkness comes, bleak winter soon begins.
The autumn trees are lined by watchful crows.

Sad graven angels twilight graveyards guard,
A twinkling forest flaming at their feet—
The thousand candles placed on graves to greet
Those souls in limbo, still from heaven barred.

Old Halloween

The jack-o'-lantern candle has diminished;
The trick-or-treaters come no more, no more.
The festival of black and orange is finished—
The world returns to how it was before.

But mark the day, eleventh of November,
The final harvest, called Old Halloween,
And let us light once more the goblin ember
That serves as beacon to a world unseen.

POEM NOTES

Pumpkin Planting

Actual, workable instructions for planting pumpkins! The basic directions in the poem should yield results, but here are a few more tips and tricks to help you along: Plant five or six seeds in a level, compost-enriched mound of soil, several inches apart, seed-points down, in a loose circle formation (which I like to call the Jack-o'-Lantern Crown). Keep soil moist, but not overly wet. When the sprouts are well established (when they have put on their third or fourth leaf), cull down to the strongest one or two plants (clip them off at the base, as pulling them up may damage the roots of the other plants). Well, that's enough to get you started!

Chant to the Pumpkin Patch Spirit

A few years ago, by the roadside, I found an abandoned gargoyle or Green Man head, cracked all through its satyr-like features, but still intact. Soon it became the official guardian of my pumpkin patch, and so has it been ever since. Every spring, around planting time, I chant my rhyme before it, and pour an offering of ale into its yawning mouth. In addition to this ritual, I also recite my "Pumpkin Planting" rhyme three times over the soil immediately after planting the seeds. Whether or not all of this has any effect, who can say, but it is my personal tradition, and it lends an air of ceremony to my spring gardening.

The Jack-o'-Lantern Trail

I have always held the persistent fancy that seasons are places—places we can visit at any time, if only we knew the hidden way. This poem portrays my vision of what the lost trail leading to the land of eternal autumn might look like.

Summer's Last Ember

A true occurrence from my garden—the green pumpkin decided to start turning orange right on the first morning of September, just in time for spooky season!

Jack-o'-Lantern Moon

Who can deny that the full moons in September and October always seem a little larger, a little more orange, and always seem to bear the goblin grin of a jack-o'-lantern.... I have noted several such moons throughout my life, and this poem is an attempt to capture the feelings they have stirred up in me.

Harvest Moon

A true and faithful account of a lovely autumn afternoon spent with Ashley Dioses two years ago. We visited the Irvine Regional Park Pumpkin Patch in Orange, California, as we do every September, per tradition, and it really was the evening of the Harvest Moon.

The Patron Wraith of Halloween

This poem was based on a character invented by artist Sam Heimer.

The Crows Alone Have Seen

This poem was inspired by the actual sense of dim fear I once felt when regarding the muscular, luxuriant vines of some Big Max pumpkins I was growing. Their nearly four foot high wall of tangled growth elicited from me the same primal reaction that a dangerous insect or wild creature might. I instinctively felt that these plants were...capable of things. The way their green, reaching tendrils wrapped around and strangled all lesser plants and objects certainly made an impression on me.

The Carver

My homage to the slasher genre, this poem was strongly inspired by the character Michael Myers from John Carpenter's groundbreaking film, *Halloween*.

Lord of Samhain

This poem was directly based on a computer-generated artwork created by writer and artist Russell Smeaton.

The Spirit of All Halloween
This poem was loosely inspired by a sculpture created by Jason McKittrick.

The Samhanach is Coming
According to Lisa Morton's *The Halloween Encyclopedia*, Samhanach is "A Scottish name for the dreadful bogies that were abroad on Hallowe'en, stealing babies and committing other monstrous crimes." After reading Lisa's excellent novella *The Samhanach*, I felt compelled and inspired to write my own piece on this obscure creature.

The Ballad of Lantern Jack
A verse retelling of an authentic New Jersey legend, as interpreted by Jason McKittrick.

The Headless Horseman
It probably goes without saying, but this piece was inspired by Washington Irving's classic tale, "The Legend of Sleepy Hollow."

The Halloween Mirror
The seed for this poem came to me while I was reading an entry in that most classic text, *The Book of Halloween*, by Ruth Edna Kelley. One day I hope to acquire a first edition copy....

The Clown Witch
This poem was inspired by the harlequinesque costumes and decorations illustrated in various issues of *Dennison's Bogie Book*.

The Circus in the Corn
This poem is equal parts inspired by the vintage John Winsch postcard titled "A Halloween Nightmare" (bearing fantastic art by Samuel Schmucker), as well as by bizarre true events that unfolded one October afternoon on Sauvie Island, just outside of Portland, Oregon. I and the

other members of the Crimson Circle (Ashley Dioses, Adam Bolivar, and D. L. Myers) happened upon what appeared to be an abandoned circus tent of some sort, in the leveled middle of a cornfield. Inside was a small stage and some hay-bales arranged for an audience, as well as other bizarre bits and decorations attesting to activities none of us could definitely fathom.

My Pumpkin Queen
This poem was inspired by a photo of Ashley Dioses holding her first self-grown pumpkin.

The Darkest Harvest
This poem is based on actual events that transpired, again, on Sauvie Island. The four members of the Crimson Circle were out in search of a pumpkin, which we would later carve and light at our collective poetry reading, during the absinthe-fueled Hippocampus Happy Hour hosted by Derrick Hussey at the H. P. Lovecraft Film Festival. (A reel of drink tickets ended up being dispensed out of its mouth!) Only a couple slight liberties were taken: We saw a frog, not a toad, and we did not actually carve our chosen pumpkin on site.

Samhain Remembered
Though I grow my own pumpkins every year, it is also an important annual tradition of mine to visit the pumpkin patch in mid-September, and pick a pumpkin from there as well. The ritual of choosing the exact perfect pumpkin from among hundreds of them is, I find, a powerful one—one that penetrates into the very mysteries of the harvest. My Halloween season begins in earnest with this annual ritual, and—of course—it is always me who carves the chosen pumpkins.

The Altar of Gourds
Any time I see a display of several gourds arranged together—such as on a hay-bale—I sense an accumulation of natural energy and vitality, and feel compelled to pay my solemn respect at those autumnal shrines.

Hallowed Powers

I was inspired to write this poem while reading the introductory chapter of *Llewellyn's Little Book of Halloween*, by Mickie Mueller.

Hymn to the Great Pumpkin

I consider this poem to be my magnum opus on the Halloween Mysteries as specifically exemplified by and practiced through the carving, keeping, and lighting of jack-o'-lanterns. It is, in essence, a poem on pumpkin worship.

The Darkly Hallowed Day

The feeling of breathless expectancy one can feel during the daytime on Halloween is often overlooked. I can still remember that electric feeling from my schooldays as a child, and have tried to capture its essence in rhyme. Even to this day, I feel it every Halloween.

The Four Trick-or-Treaters

The primal figures of the Witch, Devil, Ghost, and Skeleton, all held together by that most ubiquitous emblem of Halloween, the Jack-o'-Lantern, to me represent the most basic archetypal characters associated with the holiday. The Ghost might be omitted and covered under the Skeleton, as standing for death and the dead, as it often is in popular iconography, but I find that the figure of the Ghost is emblematic of things the Skeleton doesn't quite cover, such as the metaphorical ghost of the past—an undeniably essential element of Halloween. All together, the five characters stand for every aspect of Halloween: The Witch for magic and the supernatural; the Devil for trickery, and the threat of dark forces; the Ghost for the literal and metaphorical presences of the past; the Skeleton for death; and the Jack-o'-Lantern for tradition, the harvest, and light in dark times.

Halloween Greetings

My attempt to mimic the charming verses found on vintage Halloween postcards.

When the Owl Takes Flight

Many of my mentions of owls in my poetry were inspired by the owls that sometimes hoot outside my window, late at night, while I am writing.

Halloween Party

This poem was loosely based on an actual Halloween gathering I hosted, which did in fact include 'a pumpkin-patterned tablecloth,' a plethora of 'grinning gourds,' a 'Happy Halloween' banner, at least one mask, a dash of mystery, and plenty of tricks and treats. It was my first attempt at hosting a vintage style Halloween party, and I believe it was memorable for all involved.

Visions From Beyond the Veil

I have always felt that a proper Halloween celebration should involve some element of glimpsing beyond or penetrating the Veil, in however a fleeting fashion, so two years ago, I decided to attempt this by meditating at midnight on Halloween, in the dark. The resulting poem was woven from the raw images that came to me during that session, which were afterward written down by candlelight, anointed with Samhain oil made by Denise Dumars, and stored rolled up in a miniature orange coffin overnight, on my Halloween Altar.

ABOUT THE CONTRIBUTORS

K. A. OPPERMAN is a poet and artist hailing from southern California. In addition to his Halloween poetry, Opperman is the author of two volumes of Gothic poetry: *The Crimson Tome* (2015) and *The Laughter of Ghouls* (coming in early 2021), both published by Hippocampus Press. His work has appeared in *Midnight Under the Big Top* (Cemetery Dance Publications, 2020), *Black Wings of Cthulhu 6* (Titan Books, 2018), *Spectral Realms*, *Vastarien*, *Weirdbook*, *Weird Fiction Review*, *The Audient Void*, *Eye to the Telescope*, and many other venues.

LISA MORTON is a screenwriter, author of non-fiction books, and award-winning prose writer whose work was described by the *American Library Association's Readers' Advisory Guide to Horror* as "consistently dark, unsettling, and frightening." She is the author of four novels and 150 short stories, a six-time winner of the Bram Stoker Award®, and a world-class Halloween expert. She co-edited (with Leslie S. Klinger) the anthology *Weird Women: Classic Supernatural Fiction by Groundbreaking Female Writers 1852-1923*; forthcoming in 2020 is *Calling the Spirits: A History of Seances*. Lisa lives in Los Angeles.

DAN SAUER is a graphic designer and artist living in Oregon. In 2016, he co-founded (with editor/publisher Obadiah Baird) *The Audient Void: A Journal of Weird Fiction and Dark Fantasy*, which features his design and illustration work. Since 2017, he has worked extensively on book covers and interior art for Hippocampus Press and other publishers. His art often takes the form of surreal collage and photomontage, as pioneered by artists such as Max Ernst, J. K. Potter and Harry O. Morris.

**JOURNEY ONCE AGAIN
TO THE DARKNESS AT
SUMMER'S END**

OCTOBER GHOSTS
— AND —
AUTUMN DREAMS
MORE POEMS FOR HALLOWEEN

K. A. OPPERMAN

WITH ILLUSTRATIONS BY
DAN SAUER

COMING IN 2021

JACKANAPES PRESS

www.JackanapesPress.com
www.facebook.com/Jackanapes-Press

COMING SOON

from the author of *Diary of a Sorceress*

"...poetry from a night-blooming blossom ...
throbbing with incantatory power..."
—JOHN SHIRLEY, author of *Wetbones* and *Demons*

With illustrations by MUTARTIS BOSWELL

AVAILABLE FALL 2020

www.JackanapesPress.com
www.facebook.com/Jackanapes-Press

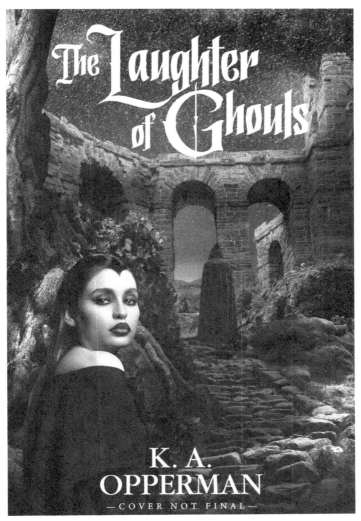 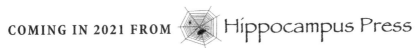

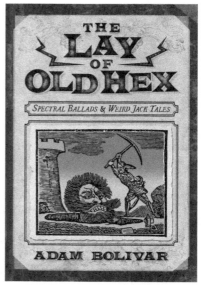

HORROR & COSMIC DAMNATION

The Crimson Tome
K. A. Opperman
Introduction by Donald Sidney-Fryer

Foreword by W. C. Farmer

*Cover art and interior illustrations
by Steve Lines*

In this scintillating volume, K. A. Opperman immediately places himself in the forefront of contemporary weird verse. Deeply influenced by Clark Ashton Smith, George Sterling, and other masters of the form, Opperman nonetheless reveals a vibrancy and originality of outlook that stamps his poetry as very much his own. A master of several of the most rigorous forms of metrical poetry— the sonnet, the quatrain, the rhyming couplet—Opperman's poetic brilliance conveys, seemingly without effort, images of terror, gruesomeness, and bleak melancholy. The book concludes with tributes to Opperman by D. L. Myers and Ashley Dioses.

Oracles from the Black Pool
D. L. Myers
Introduction by K. A. Opperman

*Cover art and interior illustrations
by Dan Sauer*

In this first book of his poetry, Myers, following the model of Lovecraft and others, has devised his own realm of weirdness, Yorehaven, with its "crouching gambrel roofs" and "maze-like streets and alleys." It is here that many of Myers's most poignant horrors find their home. While this book features vampires, werewolves, and other monsters from weird fiction's storied past, many of the creatures populating Myers's poems are of his own devising. His work uniquely lends itself to artistic representation, and noted artist Dan Sauer presents more than 20 illustrations that add a distinctive dimension to the poems.

NOW AVAILABLE FROM  Hippocampus Press

www.hippocampuspress.com

SONGS FROM THE ORANGE BOOK

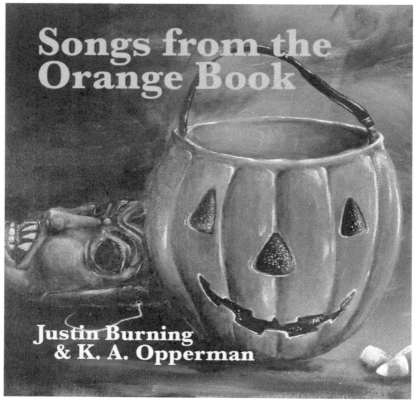

COVER ART BY MATT DOUGHERTY

THE PERFECT AUDIO COMPANION TO
PAST THE GLAD AND SUNLIT SEASON

Composer **Justin Burning** has recorded *Songs from the Orange Book*, an atmospheric album of ten poems from *Past the Glad and Sunlit Season: Poems for Halloween*. Each poem is recited by K. A. Opperman, and set to haunting music by Justin. This album is a perfect companion to *Past the Glad and Sunlit Season*, and will help set the mood for All Hallows' Eve.

The digital album is available for purchase at
jburning.bandcamp.com